26/2/20

KT-179-898

celebrate ... 2022
every child and young perso...
love books by giving you the chance to have a book of your
own. To find out more, and get great recommendations on
what to read next, visit **worldbookday.com**

World Book Day in the UK and Ireland is made possible
by generous sponsorship from National Book Tokens,
participating publishers, booksellers, authors and illustrators.
The £1* book tokens are a gift from your local bookseller.

*World Book Day works in partnership with a number of charities,
all of whom are working to encourage a love of reading for pleasure.*

The National Literacy Trust is an independent charity
that encourages children and young people to enjoy
reading. Just 10 minutes of reading every day can make a
big difference to how well you do at school and to how
successful you could be in life. **literacytrust.org.uk**

The Reading Agency inspires people of all ages and
backgrounds to read for pleasure and empowerment.
They run the Summer Reading Challenge in partnership
with libraries; they also support reading groups in schools
and libraries all year round. Find out more and join your
local library. **summerreadingchallenge.org.uk**

World Book Day also facilitates fundraising for:

Book Aid International, an international book donation
and library development charity. Every year, they provide
one million books to libraries and schools in communities
where children would otherwise have little or no opportunity
to read. **bookaid.org**

Read for Good, who motivate children in schools to read
for fun through its sponsored read, which thousands of schools
run on World Book Day and throughout the year. The money
ra... the
ch...

*(...

9030 00006 8619 0

Also available by Malorie Blackman
for young adult readers

The Noughts & Crosses sequence
NOUGHTS & CROSSES
KNIFE EDGE
CHECKMATE
DOUBLE CROSS

CHASING THE STARS
BOYS DON'T CRY
NOBLE CONFLICT
THE STUFF OF NIGHTMARES

Anthologies
LOVE HURTS
An anthology of love against the odds from the very
best teen writers, edited by Malorie Blackman

UNHEARD VOICES
An anthology of stories and poems to commemorate
the bicentennial anniversary of the abolition of
the slave trade

*For a full list of Malorie's books for readers of all ages
visit malorieblackman.co.uk*

NOUGHT FOREVER

MALORIE BLACKMAN

PENGUIN BOOKS

LONDON BOROUGH OF WANDSWORTH

9030 00006 8619 0	
Askews & Holts	29-Jul-2019
JF TEENAGE 11-14	£5.00 per set
	WW19006600

istralia

Scoth Arica

se group of companies

randomhouse.com.

vw.ladybird.co.uk

(H) | UK

First published 2019

001

Text copyright © Oneta Malorie Blackman, 2019
The Miseducation of Cameron Post text copyright © emily m. danforth, 2012

The moral right of the authors has been asserted

Set in 11/18pt Bembo Std
Typeset by Jouve (UK), Milton Keynes
Printed and bound in Great Britain by Clays Ltd, Elcograf S.p.A.

A CIP catalogue record for this book is available from the British Library

ISBN: 978–0–241–38879–2

All correspondence to:
Penguin Books
Penguin Random House Children's
80 Strand, London WC2R 0RL

MIX
Paper from responsible sources
FSC® C018179
www.fsc.org

Penguin Random House is committed to a sustainable future for our business, our readers and our planet. This book is made from Forest Stewardship Council® certified paper.

For Neil and Liz, with love

one. Dan

I've never been shot before. My shoulder hurts like a son of a bitch, as if someone is repeatedly sticking a red-hot barbed arrow into it. It's dark but I keep seeing white flashes like spots of lightning jabbing at me. Am I going into shock? Must be. But I can't pass out, not now. Then I'll be dead for sure. Where can I go to escape the wrath of McAuley's cronies? Those who are left will have regrouped by now and they'll be after me to avenge their boss. Every last one of them. If I hand myself over to the cops, I'm dead. Even if I had a passport – which I don't – if I try to escape the country,

I'm dead. If I show my face in public, I'm dead. Basically, I'm roast chicken.

This is all Tobey's fault. My so-called 'best friend' – Tobey Durbridge. He's the one who messed up, thinking he could take on a headcase like Alex McAuley on his own. I had no choice but to step in and bail him out. Trouble is, by cleaning up Tobey's mess, I'm now on the hook for it. I've got cops to the left of me, McAuley's minions to the right, all hunting me down like it's open season. That puts me right at the top of the endangered species list. Thanks, Tobey! Why should I feel a way about what happened to him? Should I beat myself up because it's my fault his life fell apart?

Not gonna happen.

Yet here I am, on the run and fighting to stay alive. My only hope is to hide until I figure out a way to disappear for good on my own terms. I'll need to change my appearance, my height, my weight. First things first. The wound in my right shoulder is bleeding like a water feature. My side is on fire – and I have no idea why. I've just had the fight of my life with McAuley and some of his allies. I didn't emerge unscathed.

Now I need to lie low.

Lightning flashes – brighter, faster, all around me. Beyond them, the darkness deepens.

Don't drop, Dan.

I fall to my knees, no longer able to stay upright. I pitch forward, hit the ground and carry on down till it feels like I must be falling right through the earth.

two. Eva

It's one of those nights. One of those nights when I sit alone in the dark at the living-room window and watch the world go by. One of those nights when, if my hatred were fuel, I would happily light a match and watch the whole world *burn*. I hate this date – the third-year anniversary. If it was a wedding anniversary, what would that be? Cotton? No, leather. A third birthday should bring cake and candles, books and toys. What does a third-year death anniversary bring? Memories and regrets and pain.

Three years.

Three long years.

Time moves forward, the world keeps turning. But not for me. Not since my Avalon died. She was so young, her whole life ahead of her, but she thought she knew it all. The occupational hazard of youth. If only I could've kept my daughter safe forever, a baby in my arms where I could protect her from the world. But parenthood is a never-ending sequence of letting go, however much you might fight against it.

And now my Ava is dead.

And those responsible are still out there, enjoying life.

And what can I do about it? Nothing. Yet another addition to my long list of failures.

Wait . . .

Who's that hanging around on the opposite side of the street?

A Nought guy wearing a woolly hat, leather jacket and jeans. He's standing beneath a streetlamp, the light reflecting off his pale skin, giving it an unhealthy sallow glow. I frown as I watch him, confident that with the living-room light off he can't see me. He's looking up and down the street like he's casually observing things, but he's acting – and badly at that. He's searching for someone specific and trying to hide that fact. I watch as he shakes his head at a figure I can only just see further along the road. Without warning, he looks in my direction. Straight at me. I draw back in my chair. He can't see me, so why do I feel the guy's eyes burning through me?

Well, he can go to hell.

And when he does, he'll find me there ahead of him.

Standing, I head for my front door and bolt it, top and bottom. This is Meadowview. Can't be too careful. Then I head for the kitchen. When I switch on the light, the sudden brightness momentarily hurts my eyes. I sigh, seeing more clearly now. My imagination is working overtime tonight. That guy opposite my house is probably just searching for his cat or something. I put on the kettle. While waiting for it to boil, I look out of the kitchen window. It's cold out there. Dark and miserable. My favourite echo. Reining in my gaze, I focus on my reflection in the window. With the kitchen lights on, I can't see much beyond it anyway. Now that my front door is locked and bolted, there's nothing outside these walls and windows but my reflection. I don't recognize the woman who always stares back at me, the creases reaching from the corners of her downturned lips to her chin, making her mouth resemble that of a ventriloquist's dummy. Frown lines plough her forehead; her cold brown eyes are like chips of ice. This reflection rarely laughs, never smiles. Life sits around her shoulders like a cloak of nettles and thorns.

It's not just life weighing me down, it's the silence around me. I head for the small TV that sits self-consciously in a corner of the work surface. Switching it on, I mute the volume. It's the only company I want or need. Then it's back to my kettle, still waiting for it to boil.

What was that?

Something . . . some*one* moving – in my back garden?

A trick of the light?

There it is again, illuminated in part by the upstairs lights of the house next door.

There is definitely someone out there, creeping around. The guy in the woolly hat?

How dare he!

This is my home, damn it! No one has the right to be in my back garden without my say so. If it's not him, it's probably another couple who think they can get busy beneath my shrubs. The perils of living next to a park. Everyone treats my garden like an extension of the public space. I'm going to douse someone's backside with freezing cold water from my garden hose if it's yet another frisky duo making out.

Then I see that it's definitely only one person – struggling to stay on their feet. A man. At least, I think so. He takes a step and stumbles. He stumbles again.

The man falls to his knees, then drops like a stone.

Not giving myself a chance to think, I grab my torch, unlock the back door and head outside. It's dark but it doesn't take me long to find him. A face I've never seen before. A Nought boy, lean and long, lying still on the grass. He groans and shifts slightly, then is still again. In the torchlight I see that he has a dark patch on his forehead and a darker patch around his stomach staining his pale shirt, exposed by his unbuttoned jacket. There's yet another stain across his right shoulder and down his right arm. Blood. I don't need my years of medical training to see that this boy is in a bad way. I have to get him inside, then I can phone for an ambulance.

'Hey. Are you all right?' Stupid question. 'Can you stand? What's your name?'

I pull at his hand. He's a dead weight and isn't shifting.

'Can. You. Stand?' I crouch down, placing my hands under and over his uninjured left arm, trying to drag him up while still holding onto the torch. The torchlight is bouncing all over the garden. I place the torch on the ground pointing straight at us and try again.

Oh great! Now it's beginning to rain. Just what I need.

Taking a deep breath, I pull at the boy. 'Stand up, damn it!' He tries to sit up, only to fall back onto the ground and roll sideways. That's when I see it – a BFG.

A big freakin' gun. I have no idea what type it is, which country made it, what calibre of bullets it takes, but one thing I do know. It's the real deal. A real gun that shoots real bullets.

Horrified, I reach out for it.

The boy gets there first.

His left hand snatches it up. He immediately turns the gun on me, his breath wheezy and pained each time he exhales. Terrified, I cross my hands in front of my face, my blood running like ice water in my veins. I focus on the gun in his hand. The whole world is now the gun in his hand.

My ass is going to get shot, sure as the earth orbits the sun.

Serve me right for trying to help this little scrotum in the first place.

'You're hurt.' I speak quietly. 'I'm a nurse. I can help.'

Or, rather, I *used* to be, but now's not the time for details.

'Get—' Cough. 'Get me up.' OK, not entirely a boy then. Not with that gravelly voice.

And what does he think I've been trying to do for the last five minutes? Grabbing the torch, I move to his side and slip my hand under his uninjured arm.

'I can't lift you on my own. You've got to put some effort in too,' I puff.

Tucking his gun into the waistband of his trousers, he uses his now free hand to get some leverage to push himself upright. The moment his hand hits the ground, he gasps in agony. So much for that idea. He tucks his legs beneath his torso and pushes upward. I can't take my eyes off that gun of his. I hope the safety is on. Actually, come to think of it, I don't. Someone should've told him that putting a gun down your trousers is a sure-fire way to get your backside or tenders shot clean off. That's a manoeuvre only used in badly researched films, not real life.

At last the boy is on his feet, with most of his weight on my shoulders. He pulls the gun out of his waistband and waves it towards my back door. That isn't rain on my forehead but sweat. Like I don't have enough to contend with already. I glance up. A face is watching from the bedroom window of the house next door. Mr Schubaker. My eyes widen at the sight of him, sending a silent message.

Call the police.

Call for help. Do something—

I drop my gaze before the boy leaning on me realizes that I'm staring up at next door's window. I don't want him to panic and start shooting. What will my neighbour do? Mr Schubaker and I are not exactly friends – or even on speaking terms. He was always having a go about Treble, my cat, doing her business in his veg patch. The first umpteen times I tried to explain to him that cats go where they want and, short of keeping her locked in the house, there wasn't a lot I could do. He wasn't happy with that explanation, to say the least. Then Treble disappeared. I let her out one night and never saw her again. And I know Schubaker had something to do with her disappearance. He and I ended up having a shouting match out in the street and we haven't spoken since. Now I'm praying he'll set aside our differences – at least to call the police. Will he see this boy and his BFG and immediately dial for help or will he decide not to get involved, especially when it comes to the authorities? Too many times we Noughts ask the police, who are mostly Cross, for help and, the next thing you know, they're tearing through our possessions demanding to see receipts for everything we own or proof of our citizenship. Can Schubaker even see us out here in my back garden?

'Move,' the boy orders. He waves his gun towards the door again, just in case I'd forgotten he had it.

We make our way into the house. I take him to one of the three chairs around my small kitchen table. The boy doesn't so much sit as collapse onto a seat. His face has a waxy sheen — it's the colour of semi-skimmed milk. Blood loss. His head slumps onto the table. Should I use the opportunity to make a grab for the gun?

Only if I want to get my fool head shot off.

Pursing my lips, I head for the sink, soak a tea towel and wring it out before returning to the intruder in my kitchen.

'I'm Eva. What's your name?' I ask.

'Dan,' he murmurs.

'Dan what?'

He raises his head to glare at me, obviously annoyed that he's volunteered even that much information. 'Dan You-don't-need-to-know-any-more,' he snaps.

'Well, Dan You-don't-need-to-know-any-more, you have to take off your hoodie and your shirt so I can clean your wounds.'

'No I don't,' says Dan with entirely too much bass in his voice.

I shrug. 'Fine. Die in agony of blood loss and infection then. No skin off my nose.'

Dropping the tea towel in the sink, I reach for the kettle and flick the switch to reheat the water. Am I about to feel a bullet rip through me? It isn't wise to turn my back on the pimple in my kitchen, but he's giving me attitude when all I want to do is clean him up. So he can go to hell too. More than ever I need a cup of strong black coffee. Maybe I'll get a sip or two down my throat before this boy decides I'm not worth the aggravation and pulls the trigger. I get myself a mug and ladle in a dessertspoon of instant coffee. Well, it's not the caffeine that's going to kill me. Not tonight at any rate.

'I'll have a cup of coffee,' says the gravelly voice behind me.

'Not without a "please" you won't,' I tell him without turning round.

'I'm the one with the gun. Remember?' God, could he sound any more pissed? I seem to have that effect on people.

'Shoot me' – I turn my head to level my gaze at him – 'and you'll have to make your own damned coffee. By the way, there are at least two men outside on the street who I've never seen before. They're probably looking for you. Go ahead and shoot me if you want them to know exactly where you are.'

Dan's eyes widen at the information. He looks like a rabbit in headlights.

'So you see,' I tell him, 'a "please" is a lot less noise and effort.'

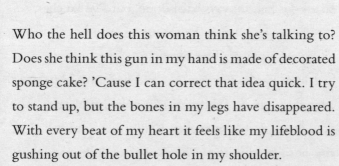

three. Dan

Who the hell does this woman think she's talking to? Does she think this gun in my hand is made of decorated sponge cake? 'Cause I can correct that idea quick. I try to stand up, but the bones in my legs have disappeared. With every beat of my heart it feels like my lifeblood is gushing out of the bullet hole in my shoulder.

'Are you going to let me clean the wound now or should I wait for you to pass out first?' asks the woman. What did she say her name was? Eva? 'You need an ambulance.'

'NO! No ambulance. Promise me—' Jesus! If she calls an ambulance, the moment they see the bullet hole they'll alert the police, and then I'm done – as in, stick-a-fork-in-me done. Out here, at least I have a chance. Once I'm a police cell, the odds on me seeing the sun rise tomorrow are non-existent.

Eva frowns. 'I'm not going to sugar-coat it. You've lost a lot of blood. You need to go to hospital.'

Her words are like a metal-booted kick to my already sore side. I feel as weak as a kitten. I hate having to ask for help, always have done, but I've no choice.

'Please, Eva. I may be dying but if you call for an ambulance I'm dead for sure.'

I look her in the eye. An overweight middle-aged Nought woman, auburn hair streaked with grey, and cold, hard, dark brown eyes. Old before her time. God, my head is spinning. The flashes of light are taking over again.

'Please, Eva. No ambulance. No police. Promise—'

Eva, the kitchen, the whole world pitches like a ship being tossed around in a storm.

'Promise me. Please?'

'I promise,' she says reluctantly.

I slump forward.
Dan, don't pass out.
Don't pass—
Don't—

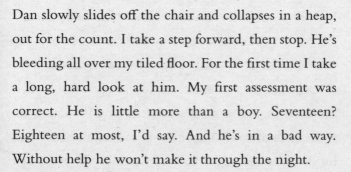

four. Eva

Dan slowly slides off the chair and collapses in a heap, out for the count. I take a step forward, then stop. He's bleeding all over my tiled floor. For the first time I take a long, hard look at him. My first assessment was correct. He is little more than a boy. Seventeen? Eighteen at most, I'd say. And he's in a bad way. Without help he won't make it through the night.

First things first.

That gun, then, promise or no promise, phone for the police.

I edge forward, waiting for Dan to spring up, grab it and cry, 'April fool!' or some such. Slowly, carefully, I reach for the pistol. Dan doesn't move. Using my thumb and index finger I pick the thing up by the grip or whatever it's called. I certainly don't want it decorating my house. No way. But where to put it?

I look around. I need to hide it until the police get here, but it can't be anywhere obvious. Less than a minute later the gun is safely salted away in my washing machine. Dan is lying on the floor, just as I left him, his eyes closed, his breathing shallow. I carefully pull off his hooded jacket and contemplate his blood-soaked long-sleeved T-shirt. There's no way I can pull that over his head. Nor do I want to. I collect my plant scissors from the window sill and head back to cut open Dan's shirt. No need to pull it off now. Retrieving the damp tea towel from the sink, I wipe the blood off his head, then his shoulder and side. The head wound is the result of a blow, probably by a fist wearing rings – or a knuckle-duster. There's a hole in Dan's shoulder which springs with fresh blood every time I clean it. He's been shot. I roll him slightly to check above his right scapula. There's a hole on the other side. The bullet went straight through.

Looks like it missed the bone, which is extremely lucky for him. I wipe his side and check that. A flesh wound. It may have been caused by a bullet but it only grazed him. It didn't enter his body. I look at his hoodie. Sure enough, there are bullet holes at the waist and shoulder. The bullet must've nicked his side and carried on out through his jacket. That one is no biggie. However, his shoulder needs urgent attention. The wound needs to be sealed or he could bleed to death. I get two compact surgical sponges out of my home-prepared first-aid kit and place them in the syringe dispenser. My kit is made up of a few high-end odds and sods 'acquired' from the hospital where I used to work. These surgical sponges are like mini, sterile, anti-bacterial tampons. Injected into a wound, they expand from the inside out, effectively sealing it and helping to fight any infection. Dan needs two of these, front and back. Once they're in place, I clean his shoulder of blood and then bandage it. It'll need careful monitoring. Then, cleaning the wound on his side, I get some gauze and tape it.

And in all this time he still hasn't moved. Not once.

I wipe the blood off my floor and strip my table. My lace tablecloth is bloody ruined. Thanks! After chucking it on top of the gun in the washing machine, I feel Dan's forehead. Cool and clammy. He's in shock and not yet out of the woods, not by any stretch of the imagination. Making myself a coffee, I contemplate the boy lying on my floor. He's lost a lot of blood but he's young and strong and should pull through – if he gets the proper medical treatment. What I should do now, of course, is call the authorities. But I can just picture it – the endless questions, the suspicions and accusations, with the police assuming that this boy is something to me, or that I had something to do with his injuries. We Noughts are always presumed guilty until proven and certified innocent. The price of a paler skin. And I remember the absolute fear and desperation clouding Dan's eyes as he pleaded with me not to call the police or for an ambulance.

I don't need to be a genius to realize that he is probably on the run – an audience with the police is the last thing he wants. Hmm! I shouldn't just leave him on my kitchen floor, but there's no way I can carry him upstairs to my spare bedroom, or even lift him onto the chair again. Besides, why should I do that? I don't owe him anything. He waved a gun in my face, for Shaka's sake!

Phone the police? It's a no-brainer.

That's *exactly* what I should do.

So why am I hesitating?

I miss my baby. I miss my Avalon.

Avalon had nothing to do with this boy. They were about the same age, but that's all they have in common. Except for their lack of judgement. But my Avalon was . . . special. She tried to see the good in everyone, only to crumble when she realized that not everyone was good. This boy is straight up trouble. The fact that he had a gun told me that much.

Enough with the wavering. I owe this boy nothing – and especially not my promises. As I turn to retrieve my phone from the hall table, where it lives when I'm in the house, an image on the TV catches my eye. Shock jolts my body as I recognize the face being broadcast.

And in that moment everything changes.

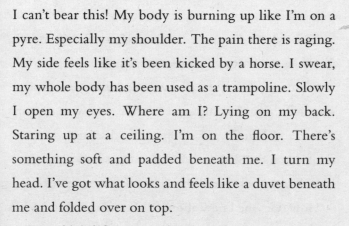

five. Dan

I can't bear this! My body is burning up like I'm on a
pyre. Especially my shoulder. The pain there is raging.
My side feels like it's been kicked by a horse. I swear,
my whole body has been used as a trampoline. Slowly
I open my eyes. Where am I? Lying on my back.
Staring up at a ceiling. I'm on the floor. There's
something soft and padded beneath me. I turn my
head. I've got what looks and feels like a duvet beneath
me and folded over on top.

'I couldn't lift you, so that was the next best thing,'
says a woman's voice. 'I had to roll you onto it. Nearly
broke my back.'

My head whips round at the sound. Even that movement makes my shoulder flare with agony.

Eva.

She's sitting on a chair, watching me. In the corner of the kitchen a small TV I didn't notice before is on, the volume low.

'Are you Dan Jeavons?'

My heart starts to ping all around my body like one of those super-balls that, once you chuck them, won't stop bouncing.

'Wh-where d'you get that name from?' My mouth feels like the bottom of a parrot's cage.

'Your face has been all over the news,' says Eva. 'I searched through your pockets while you were uncon-scious and found your phone. I've dismantled it and stomped on the SIM card. I suspect that's how your mates outside my house were able to track you so quickly.'

How does she know about SIMs and tracking? Who *is* she?

'Your friends are still hanging around, by the way,' says Eva. 'You want I should go and get them?'

'NO!' The word explodes from me.

I catch the gleam of satisfaction in Eva's eyes. With one word I've confirmed every suspicion she has about me. I purse my lips, telling myself not to say another word. Then I mentally shake my head. That's called locking the stable door after the horse has long since chilled.

'Where's my gun?' I whisper.

'Somewhere you'll never find it, so don't even bother looking. Can you stand?' asks Eva. 'I can help you up, but don't expect me to lift you.'

I nod, pushing myself up on my good arm. My head begins to whirl but I take long, slow, deep breaths. As deep as the pain in my side and shoulder will allow. I want my gun, but I don't have the energy to argue or threaten. All kinds of thoughts are rushing through my head, like: Why is this woman helping me when, before, she wouldn't have peed on me if I was on fire? And how did McAuley's minions find me so quickly? Was Eva right about the phone? McAuley had given me the mobile, just as he'd paid for the clothes on my back and the food I'd put in my stomach over the last few years. Everything I was and did since I was thirteen was thanks to him. That's when I started working for him – running errands, delivering verbal messages at first, then physical ones. As long as I looked out for McAuley and did as I was told, he looked after me. And now he's gone. If his remaining crew get hold of me, I don't doubt they'll take pleasure in thanking me for that in person.

Damn Tobey!

He's the one who said yes to delivering a package for me – and that's how all this began. No one twisted Tobey's arm. No one put a gun to his head or a knife to his ribs. It was his decision. How was I to know that there was a body part in the package? And then, because Tobey couldn't keep his mouth shut, his girl got shot. That was nothing to do with me either. Not my fault. In revenge, Tobey played the Dowds and Alex McAuley against each other like a chess grandmaster – till it all went pear-shaped. I should never have stepped in to help him.

Now death is breathing down my neck.

Being dead is nothing.

It's the dying part that scares the hell out of me.

'D'you want me to phone your family or something?' asks Eva.

I shake my head. 'I don't have any family,' I whisper. Mum won't even notice I'm gone, and my brother, Tom, is better off without me. He's too ready to follow in my footsteps as it is. Even if I get everything else wrong, I'm determined to do right by my brother, even if it means turning my back on him and walking away. He won't understand. He won't forgive me for deserting him, but I don't need his forgiveness. What I need is for him to make better choices than his older brother. The way things stand, Tom is my only hope for a better future.

With Eva's help, I finally make it onto a chair. Taking a glass out of an eye-level cupboard, she then heads for the sink and turns on the cold tap. Once the glass is full she hands it to me. I eye it, then take it from her, careful not to touch her hand. Once I start drinking I can't stop. I hadn't realized I was so thirsty.

'Another?' Eva asks as I drain the glass.

I nod.

As she refills it, I notice that the kitchen blinds are down. She turns, then follows my gaze.

'Can't be too careful, eh? We don't want any prying eyes.'

Said the spider to the fly.

Except which one of us is the predator and which one the prey?

Moments turn into minutes as we regard each other. This woman has got me completely baffled. She's looking at me like I'm something nasty she just stepped in or coughed up, so why isn't the room teeming with armed police – or at least McAuley's buddies, who are swarming on the street outside? I don't get it.

'Why're you helping me?'

Eva places the glass of water on the table in front of me. 'They say on the TV that you killed Softly McAuley. Alex McAuley, the underworld butcher. Is that true?'

That makes me start. *Softly McAuley?*

'How d'you know his nickname?' I croak. 'Only those who work for him know him . . . *knew* him by that name.'

Eva shrugs. 'Heard it somewhere.'

No, no, no. Heard it somewhere, my ass.

What's going on here?

Who *is* this woman?

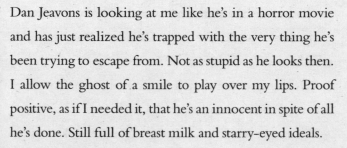

six. Eva

Dan Jeavons is looking at me like he's in a horror movie and has just realized he's trapped with the very thing he's been trying to escape from. Not as stupid as he looks then. I allow the ghost of a smile to play over my lips. Proof positive, as if I needed it, that he's an innocent in spite of all he's done. Still full of breast milk and starry-eyed ideals.

'How d'you know Alex McAuley?' Dan asks again.

'Drink your water,' I say, pointing at the glass on the table. 'You've lost a lot of blood. You need to rest and replenish your fluids. You probably need a blood transfusion. Have you changed your mind about me calling for an ambulance?'

Dan looks at me but doesn't answer. He gets the threat.

'So what were you?' I ask. 'One of McAuley's pawns? Or did the Dowds send you to McAuley to do their dirty work?'

Whatever McAuley didn't run in Meadowview, the Dowd family did. They are dark-skinned Crosses, determined to get their slice of the Meadowview pie. And they're just as ruthless as McAuley, carving their way up the status pole one ruined and wrecked body at a time.

'I don't work for the Dowds,' Dan protests, scandalized. 'I'd never work for a Cross.'

'Working for one low-life scumbag is pretty much like working for another.'

'I'd never work for a Cross.' Dan's cheeks redden as he repeats his statement. Wincing, he pulls up the sleeve covering his uninjured arm. The words *Nought Forever* are tattooed on his forearm, black writing on a fluttering white flag inside a red heart. I stare at him, surprised at how surprised I am to see his tattoo. So it's like that, is it?

'You know if you're caught with that tattoo it's a year in jail – minimum.'

'I'm not going to deny who or what I am or what I believe. I don't care who knows it,' says Dan.

Yeah, right. Then why the long-sleeved T-shirt? Members of Nought Forever are hard-line terrorists. They bomb, murder and maim indiscriminately. As long as their targets are Crosses, that's all they care about. I've seen them and their rallies on the TV, guarded by the police while decent people – Nought and Cross – shout abuse at them, but it's the first time I've actually met one in person. So that's who Dan is, or at least who he aspires to be.

I shake my head. 'I should've known. You lot are all the same.'

'*You lot?*' Dan bristles. 'What's that supposed to mean? You're a Nought too.'

'Yeah, but I'm a Nought who thinks for herself – unlike you wannabe gangsters. You wanna know who "you lot" are? You, who could do so much more with your lives? You think real power is wrapped up in guns and knives and following the path others have drawn out for you? Hell no! That's such limited thinking.'

'And where does real power lie then?' Dan sneers like I don't know what I'm talking about.

'Economic power,' I tell him straight. 'We Noughts need to have our own businesses, our own politicians, our own economic base. We need to be able to make our own wealth and to function independently of the Crosses. Beat them at their own game. Then and only then will we get an equal seat at the table. You destroy your own while those who give you the orders watch as you beg for scraps from the master's table like a whining dog. They control your thinking and you don't even realize it. You play their game and you don't even know you're playing, let alone that you're never gonna win.'

Dan frowns at me but says nothing. I know I have his attention though.

'And, worse still, people like McAuley and the Dowds have got you all convinced that the guy from the next street or the next postcode is your enemy.

They keep your thinking small. Hell, they keep it microscopic. That way they can rule you without question.'

'My mind is my own,' Dan insists quietly.

'Really? When did you leave school?'

'As soon as I could.'

'Why?'

'It didn't pay,' Dan informs me.

My questions are pissing him off but I don't care.

'Did McAuley tell you that? One of McAuley's minions? Did they regale you with stories of all the money you could be making if only you'd be smart and ditch school?'

Dan's cheeks flush red. I'm spot on. The knowledge brings no satisfaction. My smile is lemon bitter as I contemplate him. 'They said the same thing to my daughter, Avalon. Told her she belonged with them instead of falling into the Cross way of being. Told her she owed it to herself and her family to start making money as soon as possible. And when they'd hooked her on lies and promises and drugs, when they truly had her, she was passed around like a party favour on McAuley's orders.'

Dan stares at me. 'Where is she now?' he asks at last.

'Six feet under—' I choke on the reply. A ball of razor blades squats at the centre of my heart, spinning slowly but inexorably. 'Avalon took her own life and left me her journal. Placed it on my bed with a single red rose while I was at work—' I have to stop, close my eyes, take a breath before I can continue. 'Then she took an overdose. Her journal told me all I needed to know about McAuley and the life she had been dragged into.'

And so much more. Tears prick at my eyes. I turn my head, not wanting this boy to see my tears. He doesn't deserve them.

'You could be so much more. McAuley told you what you were and what you are and what you will be and, instead of thinking for yourself, you chose to believe him. Because letting someone else do your thinking for you is easier, less work, less effort.'

'That's not true—' Dan protests. He tries to raise his injured arm to point at me, but he's barely raised it a centimetre when he winces, then groans, his hand dropping back down to his side. Flashes of agony mould and twist his face as if it were wet clay.

'That's not true,' he whispers again as the pain in his shoulder subsides.

'No? How many of your own kind have you ruined on McAuley's orders?' I ask. 'How much did he have to pay you to turn you into one of his sheeple? I bet it didn't even run into triple digits. You sold yourself for a couple of threats and a handful of empty promises. You're nothing but a cliché. At least McAuley did what he did because he believed in something – himself and money. What's your excuse?'

seven. Dan

The expression on Eva's face is pure poison. If it could be bottled, it could be sold as a lethal weapon. I feel her toxic glare running through my veins, racing around my brain, pumping out of my heart. I hear — and feel — every word she's saying. To my surprise, as badly as my body hurts, her words hurt more. Memories flood in like a tsunami, overwhelming me. Snapshots of my life so far.

Watching Mum try to hold down two jobs until fatigue and worse wore her down. She stopped fighting, turning into something I didn't even want to name. I'd watched her as I was growing up, swearing I wouldn't end up like her. Watching Tom cry because our house was always cold and the fridge was always empty. Living on beans on toast, or sometimes just toast, for weeks on end when money was non-existent. School was a bust. At least the reading part was. I'd look at words on a page and they wouldn't stay still, they swam around like tadpoles, and I'd been too ashamed to tell anyone. I was good at maths – I knew my times tables by heart before anyone else in my class and mental arithmetic was my thing. But there are no exams for mental arithmetic. All tests and exams involved reading and writing. So, instead of admitting that I needed help, I took the easier option: I quit and dropped out.

And buried deep the fact that I felt such a loser.

Eva is right. I *am* a cliché. I thought I was spreading my wings, doing something with my life. What a joke! Is that why I feel such antipathy towards Tobey, even though he's supposed to be my friend? Because he managed to avoid McAuley and this farce of a life until I dragged him down to wade through crap alongside me? Is that the reason I helped him when it came down to choosing him or McAuley? Guilt? A recognition of what I might've been if I'd had the guts to follow Tobey's example and think for myself?

I've been played. But the worst thing of all is, I played myself.

Slowly Eva shakes her head as she watches a whole playlist of emotions dance across my face.

'Come on. You need to lie down,' she says, finally cutting me some slack. 'D'you think you can make it upstairs?'

Being honest, I shake my head.

'Can you make it to the living room? You can lie down on the couch and get some sleep. You can't stay in the kitchen.'

I stand. With my good arm over Eva's shoulder, I finally make it to the living-room door, by which time we're both sweating.

'Stay there,' she says, leaning me against the door frame. 'I need to close the curtains.'

Once that's done, she helps me over to the couch and I collapse onto it, the last of my strength now gone.

Every bone in my body has disappeared – to be replaced by a skeleton of flame and pain.

A knock at the front door, as unexpected as it is unwelcome.

McAuley's friends. I know it. I *feel* it.

Eva frowns. 'Stay put.'

A strange, unexpected sense of calm washes over me. The whole evening, my whole life has been leading up to this moment. All the choices, the decisions, the selfish justifications have led me right here.

'Listen, Eva,' I sigh. 'Let me just go to them. There's no reason for you to get caught up in my mess.' That had happened to too many people already.

'Stay. Put,' she repeats, and she heads out into the hall.

Like I could move anyway. I'm not going anywhere. Not without help.

My entire fate rests in the hands of a woman who hates my guts.

 **eight. Eva**

'Who is it?' I call out.

'Police, ma'am. Could you open the door please?'

Police, is it? Hmm ... Through the frosted pane of glass in my door I see the silhouette of a man. And from the smooth appearance of the top of his head, he's wearing a woollen hat. Not your standard police uniform.

'What's this about, Officer?'

'There's an escaped criminal in the area and we're going door to door to make sure everyone is safe and accounted for. If you'd just open the door . . .'

'I live alone and everything's locked. I'm fine,' I tell him.

A moment's silence.

'Nevertheless, if you could just open the door please?'

The 'officer' sounds real keen to get into my house. Too keen.

'Could you put your warrant card through the letterbox please, so I can check your ID?' I ask.

Another, longer, pause.

'I don't have it on me.'

Seriously? *Seriously?*

'Come back when you do,' I say.

'Ma'am, I must insist you open this door—'

'And I must insist you sod off before I call the real police,' I shout. 'You think I'm stupid? You think I arrived in Meadowview yesterday? I let you in and you tie me up and burgle the place while I watch helplessly? Or worse. Bugger off!'

The man outside starts knocking on my door again. I head back into the living room. Now that it's a choice between those outside and the injured boy on my couch, suddenly there's no contest.

'Dan, get up!' I hiss.

He struggles, but he's so weak he can barely sit, never mind stand. So that's not going to work.

'Get on the floor,' I tell him.

With my help he rolls onto the carpet, groaning softly. The pounding on my door makes me wince, echoing what my heart is doing in my chest. The guy outside is now trying to kick it in. My ordered life of nothing touching me and me touching no one has blown up in my face. What the hell am I doing? I must be nuts. If I get caught with Dan, we're both dead for sure.

I pick up the cushions and drop them on the floor. Then I lift the base of the couch to reveal the space underneath. It's meant to be extra storage space but I never use it.

'Get in there, Dan, and keep quiet,' I say.

He doesn't need to be told twice. In one last desperate act, he raises himself up onto his knees and one hand. He and I struggle to get him inside. The moment he's fully in, he looks up at me without saying a word. His grey eyes hold both threat and entreaty. In that moment I hold his whole world in my hands, and we both know it. I bring the metal slatted seat base down on his back and put back the cushions.

Quickly I head out into the hall to call the police.

Too late.

My door slams back against the wall and the man who'd been across the street fills the door frame, glowering at me.

I'm in deep, deep manure.

'How dare you!' I exclaim, washing down my fear with a shot of anger. 'How dare you break into my house!'

Now there's another Nought man behind him, dark hair and a trim beard. Thug number one and thug number two. Police officers, my ass. McAuley's men. No doubt about it. I know gangsters when I see them. Enough of them passed through the hospital where I used to work, looking to be patched up from this fight or that stab wound.

'If you know what's good for you, you won't get in our way,' says thug one.

'Ooh! Aren't you big and brave, threatening a lone woman half your size and twice your age. Your mother must be so proud,' I say with disdain.

Both shitheads move into my hall. I stand in the living-room doorway. Thug one points up the stairs. Thug two heads up to search for their target. Thug one pushes past me into the living room. He looks around. I make sure to keep my eyes on him, not the couch. He pushes past me again to search the kitchen and the downstairs loo. Thug two comes running down the stairs, shaking his head at the silent question asked by his colleague.

'What about my door? Who's going to pay for that?' I ask.

Thug one takes out a wad of cash and throws it at me. I don't try to catch it, instead letting it fall to the floor like confetti. Like I would touch their blood money. My unwelcome guests head out, leaving my door wide open. I move behind them to close it. The lock and the bolts are busted but at least the door is still intact. I put on the chain – the only thing left that still works.

Bastards!

Sirens! And the sound is getting closer. All thanks to my nosy neighbour Mr Schubaker, no doubt. Where seeing me with a strange guy in my garden hadn't worked, obviously those creeps kicking in my door had finally made him call the police. Jesus, it's all go! Through the small frosted-glass panel in my front door I see the whirl of flashing lights. The police – the real police this time – have pulled up outside my house.

What do I do now?

If I hand Dan over to them, I don't doubt that he'll be dead inside a week. McAuley's men will find a way to get to him or they'll bribe some crooked copper to do it. If I don't hand him over and he gets better, what's to stop him finding his gun in my washing machine and turning it on me, or using one of my kitchen knives to cut my throat? Or suppose I don't hand him over and he dies on me? Two deaths on my conscience.

I can't have two deaths on my head. I'd never survive.

What am I thinking of?!

Dan isn't my problem, and I can't, I *won't*, make him my problem.

He'll have to take his chances, just like the rest of us.

But he reminds me of my daughter, rushing to be older, do supposedly better. So naïve.

Maybe if I look after Dan and see him through this, I'll somehow be atoning for not trying harder with my daughter. I should've fought to find a way to get through to her.

What should I do?

The doorbell rings.

This time I open the door to two uniformed Cross police officers, a man and a woman. The real deal.

'Officers,' I say, 'I was just about to phone you.'

Here's a sneak preview of

CROSSFIRE

the next book in the
Noughts & Crosses series,
which will be coming out
in summer 2019

Enjoy!

NOW

one. Callie

A Nought woman, no doubt some poor jobbing actress desperate to pay her rent, was kneeling down in the middle of a stylized pigsty. She held leads attached to twelve decorated sculptures of life-sized pink pigs surrounding her like the petals of a flower, all looking out at the audience. Some of the pigs wore clothes – military uniforms, or just a hat or shoes. Two of them were simulating copulation. The Nought woman wore a bodysuit that at first glance made her look naked. She was kneeling, her head down. At random intervals she looked up to stare at the person directly in front of her for a few seconds before slowly bowing her head again.

Now it was my turn to receive her numb stare. My lips twisted in distaste. Blinking rapidly, the exhibit lowered her head, her cheeks reddening.

Embarrassed for both of us, I said quietly, 'The look on my face wasn't aimed at you. It was aimed at this ridiculous so-called art installation.'

The woman's head remained bent, the slight tensing of her shoulders and her reddened face the only indications that she'd heard my words. Whether or not she believed them was another matter.

I shook my head, sighing inwardly. It had taken me years to cultivate my poker face, but there were moments – like now – when the mask slipped. After glancing at my watch I took a seat at one end of the gallery and looked around. A huge sign hanging above all the exhibits declared: ALBION – LESSONS LEARNED: A 21ST-CENTURY RETROSPECTIVE. Talk about the chieftain's new robes. This was supposed to be the most avant-garde, exciting art exhibition currently in the capital. Nought actors and actresses adorned the various works of art, a few of them naked, some covered from head to toe in body paint of various hues. They sat in, on or among the exhibits, seldom moving. The whole thing had a melancholy air of crass awkwardness to it.

If I were an art critic, I know how my review would read: *Dubious style and precious little substance.* The few articles I'd read about this so-called exhibition described it as 'daring', 'innovative', 'a fresh take' – blah blah.

Yeah, right.

Sauley J'Hara, the Cross artist responsible for this hot mess, had been all over the news during the last two weeks, responding to the very vocal criticism of his art installation.

'It's a forward-thinking look at how we used to regard and treat Noughts juxtaposed with how they are regarded now,' he'd argued.

I shook my head again. What a steaming pile of horse manure. A self-congratulatory exercise in nostalgia for the backward thinkers who wished – or still believed – they lived in the past.

I looked up at the ceiling. Now *there* was real art. Panels depicting Zafrika's history – some carved from wood, some from marble, some just painted, but all exquisitely beautiful. I glanced down at my watch again. It hadn't been my choice to meet here and I was burning to leave. The ceiling, which was part of the fabric of the building, I admired. The rest of the exhibition was making my skin itch.

'Hello, Callie. What's what?'

The baritone voice beside me made my head snap up.

Tobey Durbridge.

Damn it! My heart jumped at the sight of him, dragging me to my feet. God, it had been so long. Too long. When did the air get so thin in here? There was no other explanation for the way my heart was thumping or for feeling this light-headed.

Oh, come on! You're a grown woman, for God's sake. Get a grip, Callie Rose!

It was such a long time since Tobey and I had last met. A lifetime ago. What had I been expecting, because this wasn't it. Over the years, just like the rest of the country

I'd seen Tobey on the TV as he rose in prominence as the first elected Mayor of Meadowview, but seeing him in person was so different. Tobey had moved on and up – the only directions he was ever interested in. He was currently in a race to become the capital's first Nought mayor, and there wasn't a single soul in not just Britain but the whole of Zafrika who didn't know his name. I'd already voted, and by this time tomorrow all the smart money reckoned Tobias Durbridge would be the next Mayor of London. And that was just the start. As Solomon Camden, my head of chambers, had put it, 'Only a fool would bet against Tobey Durbridge becoming the first Nought Prime Minister of the entire country.'

And how had I voted?

Well, I was nobody's fool.

It'd been so long, too long since I'd last seen him, but I would've known this man anywhere. The Tobey of old, with his chestnut-brown hair and darker brown eyes, still stood in front of me, but his face was harder and his lips were thinner, and the gleam in his eyes, like he was constantly on the verge of a smile – well, that had all but vanished. Something told me it would take a lot to make Tobey smile these days. And he'd filled out. He was not just taller but broader. He made me feel like I was slacking on the body-conscious front. Which I was, I admit it. I enjoyed my food! I hit the treadmill regularly, but only so I wouldn't have to buy a whole new wardrobe every six months. Besides, I had my mum's ass and it was going nowhere, no matter how much I exercised. Tobey, on the other hand, wore his charcoal-grey suit like a second skin. That hadn't come off a hanger in a department store. His suit screamed bespoke from the rooftops. His black shoes didn't have a scuff mark on them, his white shirt was spotless, as was his silk purple tie. Damn! He was wearing the hell out of every stitch he had on. Instead of looking staid and boring, he managed to make the whole ensemble look . . . dangerous. Like this guy could quite easily hand you your head if you messed with him, and still look fine doing it. Aware that I was staring, I mock sighed. 'For Shaka's sake! I see you're still taller than me.'

A shared smile – and just like that the tension between us lifted.

We grinned at each other as the years began to fall away, but then reality rudely shoved its way between us. Another moment as we regarded each other. My mind was racing. Should we kiss? Hug? What? I moved forward at the same time as Tobey. A brief, awkward kiss on the lips was followed by a long hug. The warmth of his body and the subtle smell of his aftershave enveloped me. I stepped back. The moment for anything deeper, anything more, came and went, and faded away unclaimed.

'It's so good to see you, Tobey.' I felt faintly foolish that I'd had such a visceral reaction to him. 'How are you?'

Tobey opened his mouth, only to close it without saying a word. An eyebrow quirked, followed by that wry smile of his. 'I was going to say *All the better for seeing you*, but you deserve more than cheesy lines and platitudes.'

Momentarily thrown, I wondered how exactly I was meant to respond to that?

Tobey indicated the seat behind us. He waited for me to sit before parking himself next to me, his thigh pressing lightly against mine. His warmth was unsettling in its familiarity. I slowly moved my thigh so we were close but no longer touching.

Time for a change of subject. 'I was sorry to hear about you and Misty.'

'Were you? I thought you'd be pleased, as in overjoyed,' said Tobey.

Stung, I said, 'Why? D'you think I'm so petty that I'd jump up and down with glee at the news of your break-up? Seriously?'

Thanks a lot.

'You did warn me that I was making a mistake.' Tobey shrugged. 'And more than once.'

My cheeks burned. Not some of my finer moments. 'I was wrong to do that. One of my many regrets when it comes to you – and us.'

'Oh? What else d'you regret?' Tobey asked quietly.

I might have known he'd leap all over that one. No way was I going near it.

'How's your family?' I asked.

'They're fine. How's Troy?' said Tobey.

I shrugged. 'Same as ever. He manages to work my last nerve every time we meet.'

Tobey smiled. 'Isn't that what all brothers are meant to do to their sisters?'

'Troy works extra hard at it. He's seventeen, so he's at the age when he knows *everything*. God knows I love my brother, but he's hard work.'

'And your mum? Sephy?'

'She's fine. Still running the club,' I replied.

Tobey nodded. 'I was sorry to hear about what happened to Nathan.'

'Thanks.'

'I mean it. I meant to get in touch, but . . . you know how it is.'

Yeah, I knew exactly how it was. We were old friends who shared painful memories – and hurt. How much easier to let our friendship simmer at a distance rather than boil away to nothing or, worse still, turn to ice between us.

'Is it worth me apologizing again for what happened?' asked Tobey, not looking at me but at the people milling about in the gallery.

'Tobey, let it go. I have.' Which wasn't quite true, but it would do. 'Is that why you asked me to meet you here? To rehash old times?'

'No. That's the last thing I want,' Tobey replied, looking directly at me.

As we regarded each other, I felt yet another crack ripple through my heart for what might have been. So many wasted years, so much wasted time.

'Why did you want to meet here of all places?' I had to ask as I took another look around.

'Restaurant tables can be bugged. Outdoor listening devices have a range of a hundred metres and more; some can hear through walls. Museums and art galleries tend to have scanner jammers and disruptors built into the building's fabric so that no one can bypass their security and steal the contents. When I want a truly private conversation, this is where I come as it's close to my office.'

'Oh, I see.'

Nothing to do with the current exhibition then, I realized.

'I'm surprised to see you alone. Don't you have minders?' I couldn't quite believe that Tobey wandered the streets and went where he liked without bodyguards and backup. God knows there'd been enough threats against his life by the headbangers who believed being the mayor of anything and being a Nought should be mutually exclusive. There were even some Nought nutjobs who considered Tobey a traitor for engaging in what they considered 'Cross politics'.

'They're here, don't worry.' Tobey gave a faint smile.

Ah! I should've known. There had to be upwards of fifty people in the gallery, but Tobey didn't seem concerned. That meant his close-protection detail had to be top drawer. So good, in fact, that, as I looked around the room, I had to work at guessing who they might be – there had to be more than one. There was a woman studiously regarding the painting to my right. I'd put money on her being one of Tobey's bodyguards – or close-protection officers, as they preferred to be known. I continued to look around. A suited man by one of the middle installations kept throwing careless glances in our direction. He was definitely another. I had a nose for them, like I had a nose for undercover cops and guilty clients.

And the nose didn't lie or steer me wrong. Well, not usually!

Tobey and I were getting some curious glances – Tobey more than me. He was instantly recognizable. Famous and powerful – a killer combination. In the years since school, any doors that hadn't opened for him automatically Tobey had kicked in. Hard.

'So why did you want to see me after all this time?' I asked. 'On today of all days I'd have thought you had better things to do. Shouldn't you be off being interviewed to within a centimetre of your sanity?'

'I should, but I need you, Callie. Look, I'd love to play catch-up and then honey-coat this, but I don't have time.' Tobey sighed. He took a deep breath, looking into my eyes. 'The thing is . . . I . . . Well, I need your help.'

I bit the inside of my cheek to suppress a grin. 'Wow. Those are obviously some rusty words.'

'Huh?'

'You're not used to asking for help, are you?' I teased.

Tobey's smile faded as quickly as it had arrived. 'You're right, but I really do need you. The thing is – in the next week or so I'm going to be arrested for murder and I need a good lawyer. The best. And that's you.'

What?

Well, damn! Whatever I'd been expecting, that wasn't it.

I stared. 'Who are you supposed to have killed?'

Tobey didn't flinch, didn't look away. He didn't even blink. 'Daniel Jeavons.'

My eyes were starting to hurt from staring so hard. A super-surreal conversation in an unconventional setting. Come to think of it, there was no better place for this revelation.

'Dan? Dan is dead?'

Tobey nodded.

Daniel Jeavons, 'ex' criminal and shady AF king-maker, was dead. Stunned, I tried to process what I'd just heard.

Dan was dead.

'Did you do it?' I asked, the words falling out of nowhere.

The art gallery, the capital, the country, the whole world fell away until there was just Tobey and me watching each other – and the question pushing, pulsing between us.

Have you read Malorie Blackman's
award-winning, ground-breaking
Noughts & Crosses series?
Soon to be a BBC TV series!

MALORIE BLACKMAN

Noughts + Crosses

TV SERIES TIE-IN EDITION
SPRING 2019

'Intensely moving'
Carousel

'THOUGHT-PROVOKING'
The Bookseller

'Written with passion'
Sunday Times

'Dramatic, moving and brave'
Guardian

'UNFORGETTABLE'
Independent

'Blackman is a terrific thriller writer'
Evening Standard

Read on for a breathtaking extract from

THE MISEDUCATION OF CAMERON POST

'Funny, heartbreaking, and beautifully rendered . . . a new classic' Curtis Sittenfeld

'A tremendous achievement' Sarah Waters

'An important book – one that can change lives' Jacqueline Woodson

A story of love, desire, pain, loss – and, above all, finding the courage to live life according to your own rules.

The night Cameron Post's parents died, her first emotion was relief. Relief they would never know that hours earlier she'd been kissing a girl.

Desperate to 'save' her niece, Cameron's aunt takes drastic action, and sends her to a religious 'correctional' facility. Now Cameron must battle with the cost of being her true self, even if she's not completely sure who that is.

By an hour outside of Miles City, Ruth had already given up on lecturing me on appreciating *God's gift of a facility like this right in my own state*. I think she had given up on instilling in me a positive attitude before we even got on the road, but she quoted some scripture and walked through her lines as though she had written her little speech out beforehand. And knowing Ruth, she probably had—maybe in her daily prayer journal, maybe on the back of a grocery list. Ruth's words were so stale by that point that I didn't even hear most of them. I looked out my window with my nose tucked into my shoulder and smelled Coley. I was wearing one of her sweatshirts even though it was too hot for it. Ruth thought it was mine or she would have piled it into the cardboard box with the other things of Coley's, of ours, that she and Crawford had confiscated, many of those things items from our friendship and not necessarily from whatever it was that we'd become those last few weeks: snapshots, lots of them prom-night pictures; notes written on lined paper and folded to the size of fifty-cent pieces; the thick wad of rubber-banded movie tickets, of course those; and also a couple of pressed thistles, once huge and thorny and boldly purple, now dried and feathery and the ghost of their original color, dust in your hand if you squeezed too hard, and Ruth did. The thistles I'd picked at Coley's ranch, hauled back into town, and tacked upside down to the wall above my desk. But the sweatshirt, buried at the bottom of my laundry basket beneath clean but not-yet-folded beach towels and tank tops, had escaped. It still smelled like the kegger campfire at which she'd last worn it and something else I couldn't place, but something unmistakably Coley.

For miles and miles I just let Ruth drone. I let her words crumble away between us, drop like those thistles into dusty bits on the seats and the console. All the while I smelled Coley, and thought Coley, and wondered when I would start hating Coley Taylor, just how long it would take for that to happen, because I wasn't anywhere near that place yet, but I thought that maybe I should be. Or that maybe I would be one day. Eventually Ruth stopped talking to me and twisted the dial until she found Paul Harvey and laughed like she was drunk and had never heard mild radio humor before.

Those whole six hours, the only other snips of dialogue between us, other than the Pringles incident, were:

RUTH: Please roll up your window; I have the AC on.
ME: And this affects me how?

RUTH: I wish you would stop slumping like that. You're rounding your shoulders and you'll end up an old lady with a hump.

ME: Good. It will go nicely with the horns I'm
working on.

RUTH: I know that you read your manual, Cammie;
I saw you. It says you have to enter Promise
with a teachable heart if you want this to work.

ME: Maybe I don't have a heart, teachable or
otherwise.

RUTH: Don't you want this to work? I just can't
understand why anyone would want to stay
like this if they knew they could change.

ME: Stay like what?

RUTH: You know exactly what.

ME: No I don't. Say it.

RUTH: Stay in a life of sinful desire.

ME: Is that the same category for premarital sex?

RUTH: (Long pause.) What is that supposed to mean?

ME: I wonder.

Only a few miles before the turnoff to Promise we
passed the sign for Quake Lake. It was battered and the

metal was crunched in the middle, as though it had fallen down and been driven over by a semi and then put back up. I think Ruth and I noticed it at right the same time, and she turned to me, actually took her eyes from the road to look at me, for just a few seconds. But Ruth somehow managed not to say anything. And I didn't say anything. And then we turned a corner and it was just trees and road in the rearview and that sign wasn't some big signifier at all, but just one more place marker we'd driven by on our way. At least that's what we both pretended right then.

The girl who met us in the Promise parking lot had an orange clipboard, a Polaroid camera, and a prosthetic right leg (from the knee down). She seemed about my age, high school for sure, and she waved that clipboard while walking toward the FM with surprising speed. Maybe I shouldn't have been surprised: She was wearing running shorts.

Ruth didn't even have the chance to say something like "Oh, lookit this poor thing" before the poor thing herself was at Ruth's door, throwing it open and flashing a picture, all in what seemed to me the same moment.

Ruth made a gaspy-squeaky sort of noise and shook her head back and forth and blinked her eyes the way one of the *Looney Tunes* did after smacking into a brick wall.

"Sorry about the shock. I like to get one right away," the girl told us, letting the big black camera hang around her neck, pulling her head down some. The photo slid forward like a tongue, but she didn't pull it free. "Just as soon as folks get here I snap one. It has to be the very first moment; it's the best."

"Why's it the best?" I asked her, walking around the Fetus Mobile to see that leg up close. Her real one was bony and pasty white, but the fake one had some girth, some plasticky definition, and was Beach Barbie tanned.

"You can't use words to describe it—that's why the photos. I think it's because it's the purest moment. The most undiluted." Ruth did a weird kind of chuckle after she'd said that. I could tell she was uncomfortable with this girl as our greeter. The girl finally plucked free the picture and held it up so only she and I could see it. The shot was mostly Ruth's head too close to the lens and her mouth a line of displeasure, with me seeming far behind her, almost smiling.

"I'm Cameron," I said. I knew that if I didn't speak, Ruth would, and for some reason I wanted this girl to like me right away. Maybe because whoever it was I had been expecting to meet us, this girl wasn't her.

"I know. We've all been talking about you coming. I'm Jane Fonda." She was smiling and rocking a little on that leg. It squeaked like a bath toy.

"Serious? Jane Fonda?" I smiled back.

"I'm always serious," she said. "Ask anybody. So the deal is that Rick's in Bozeman at Sam's Club buying food and stuff. I'll give you the grand tour and then he'll be back before too long." She leaned toward me. "Sam's Club and Walmart give us a big discount, and free food, sometimes. Mostly chicken breasts and bananas. He does a decent barbecue chicken, but he gets the cheap toilet paper—the scratchy kind you have to double up on."

"There are worse things," Ruth said. "Shall we bring the luggage now?"

"Indubitably," Jane said.

"I can't believe your name is actually Jane Fonda," I said. "That's crazy."

She tapped her clipboard against her leg two times and it sounded sorta like when I was little and would tap my plastic drumsticks against my Mr. Potato Head. "Talk about the tip of the iceberg," she said. "We swim in crazy here."

• • •

The grounds at Promise had a little of everything that western Montana is famous for, things that the state tourism board makes sure show up on postcards and in guidebooks: golden-green fields for archery or horseback riding, densely wooded trails dotted with Indian paintbrush and lupine, two streams that, according to Jane, were just *aching with trout*, and a so-blue-it-looked-fake mountain lake only a mile and a half's hike away from the main building. Both sides of the campus (the compound) were bordered by the grazing land of cattle ranchers sympathetic to the holy cause of saving our souls from a lifetime of sexual deviance. Even that hot August afternoon, the wind down from the mountains was crisp, and on it rode the sweet scent of hay, the good spice of pine and cedar.

Jane Fonda took us cross-country, that squeaky leg surprisingly springy, and Ruth determined not to lose step with a cripple, even if not losing step meant bouncing the battered, green, Winner's-Airlines-issued wheelie suitcase now packed with my stuff over prairie-dog holes and sagebrush. I lugged a pink Sally-Q case, one that Ruth had told me she would be taking back with her, but I could keep the Winner's one. Out with the old, in with the new.

Jane sort of motioned to the chicken coop (eggs were collected each morning by students on a rotating schedule); to an empty horse stable (they were planning to get some horses, though); to a cluster of metal-roofed cabins used only during the summer, for camp; to two small cabins where Reverend Rick and the school's assistant director, Lydia March, lived. But Jane wasn't so much a tour guide as someone we might have happened upon in a foreign town, someone who felt obligated to show us around a little. As we walked, I stared at the back of her T-shirt. On it was a black-and-white print of a female athlete, maybe a volleyball player, judging by her shorts and tank top, stretching after an exhausting match—her ponytail limp, her brow dewy. Next to the image were the purple words SEEK GOD IN ALL THAT YOU DO.

The main building was built, I think, to resemble an aspen lodge, with log siding and a grand entrance; but once we were inside, it felt just like Gates of Praise back in Miles City, but bigger, and with dorm rooms. The floors were all that industrial laminate poorly imitating hardwood. The windows were too few, fluorescent lighting everywhere. Someone had made an attempt with the main room—a fireplace, cheap Navajo-style woven rugs, a moose head over the mantel—but even that room smelled like disinfectant and floor cleaner.

"Where is everybody?" I asked, and was first answered by a cavernous echo of my own voice.

"Most everybody's in Bozeman with Pastor Rick. Lydia's somewhere in England—that's where she's from. She visits a couple times a year. But I think some disciples are at the lake, maybe. Summer camp just ended last week, so this is like transition time before the regular school session starts. Freedom time." She flicked on a light switch and started down a hallway.

"So you kids just do whatever you want this week?" Aunt Ruth trot-trotted a little to catch her, the suitcase wheels spinning sprays of dirt and grass on those shiny floors.

"I mean not really. We just don't have as many group activities, but we still do our Bible study and one-on-one sessions." She stopped at a closed door, which had two things taped to it: a poster of the Christian rock band Audio Adrenaline and a Xerox copy of the Serenity Prayer, the purple ink so faded and the paper so yellowed and curled that it somehow had gained an air of history, almost of authenticity.

Jane tapped the door with her clipboard. "This is you. And Erin. She's in Bozeman with Rick."

Aunt Ruth *tsk-tsk*ed her head some. She still hadn't come to terms with the roommate thing. Who could blame her? I hadn't either. I'd been given her name earlier in the week and I'd been regularly picturing my new roommate, Erin, as a bespectacled, chubby girl with unruly curls and a smattering of acne across her perpetually flushed cheeks. Erin would be a pleaser. I just knew it. She would be working hard, asking God to help her so that the grungy but holy men in that poster on our door might actually do it for her—goose bumps on her neck, a prickle across her chest. Praying to Jesus to help her want them the way she had that girl from her study hall, from her science lab. *He's a tall drink of water* she would tell me about some male movie star, some action hero, and then she would giggle. Erin would most definitely be a giggler.

We were still waiting outside the door. Jane nodded at the handle. "You can go in," she said. "We don't lock anything here. The doors aren't usually even shut, but since no one's in there, it's fine, I guess." She must've seen my face because she added, "You'll get used to it."

I couldn't quite believe her.

Erin's half of the room was done up in lots of yellows and purples: a yellow bedspread with purple pillows, a purple lamp with a yellow shade, a massive bulletin board with a yellow-and-purple-striped frame, the whole thing collaged with snapshots and Christian concert tickets and handwritten Bible quotes.

"Erin's from Minnesota. Big Vikings fan," Jane said. "Plus she's a second year, and she's earned some privileges you don't have, I mean with the posters and whatever." She looked at me, shrugged her shoulders. "Yet. You'll get them eventually. Probably, anyway."

My half of the room was sterile and blank, and I hadn't really brought much to change that. We put my bags on the new-looking twin mattress. I wasn't sure if I was supposed to unpack right then, so I just pulled out a few random items and set them on my desk hutch: a stack of brand-new notebooks and a box of pens, purchased by Ruth; Kleenex; a picture of Mom and Dad and me one Christmas; Mom's pre–Quake Lake picture; the picture of Margot and Mom, which Ruth had looked at sort of funny while inspecting my luggage but had let me keep. *Make an effort,* I thought. I added my *Extreme Teen Bible.*

Ruth was examining that big bulletin board. She seemed to be noticing my lack of color in the face of all that was the Viking Erin. Maybe it made her a little sad for me. She reminded me to grab the reading lamp and alarm clock from the Fetus Mobile before she left with them.

"I think you're going to do really well here, Cammie. I mean it." She reached out to put an arm around me and I stepped away from her, pretending that I had a sudden and compulsive interest in looking out the window I'd be looking out all year. The view was unbelievable, so there was that, anyway.

Thank God Jane got us out of there. "Would you like to stop by the dining hall? Rick thought you might be hungry. There's sandwich stuff."

"Sounds good," Ruth said, already out the door.

Jane squeaked fast behind her. I paused at the bulletin board. There was one girl repeated in every photo. Had to be Erin. I was right about everything but the acne. Her skin was as clear as those girls in Noxzema ads, maybe due to her prayers before lights out. *God grant me flawless pores. God grant me a healthy glow.*

• • •

We were only just finished with egg salad on white when a big blue van pulled up outside, and the sliding door with the silver God's Promise logo slid open, and my fellow diseased poured out like a rush of holy water to pass over me and cleanse me and envelop me into their stream.

It was *Hi, I'm Helen. We're just so glad that you're here.* And *I'm Steve. We just bought tons of Cap'n Crunch. Are you into Cap'n Crunch? So good.* And Mark and Dane said they'd show me the lake, and Adam said he'd heard that I was a runner, and that he ran in the mornings and had seen tons of elk and deer and even a moose once or twice. *And those things are freakin' huge.* And it was these tight little embraces, and touching my arm, and these shiny, shiny eyes, and everyone smiling at me like we were all plastic characters out of some board game like Candy Land or Hi Ho! Cherry-O. And the thing I kept thinking was: *Is it really okay to be doing all this touching?*

I looked at Jane, who seemed just as royally awkward, that camera still hanging from her neck, and I checked to make sure, in all this goodness and light, that her fake leg hadn't suddenly healed itself, sprouted anew and perfect and pure. It hadn't. That was something.

The Viking Erin was the last off the van. She stepped from it like it was a carriage once sprung from a pumpkin, all these bright-eyed well-wishers her subjects, her court, and me the new lady-in-waiting. She was confident in her denim overalls and sandals, her curls shiny and healthy; everything about her— even her roundness, her softness—made her seem somehow healthy. Maybe I was totally wrong about this girl. Maybe she was their leader?

She shrieked when she saw me. And then the giggle, a trajectory of such giggles. As we hugged, she said everything that prayer on her door, that bulletin board, had told me she would. How she was so glad to again have a roommate, and so glad we would take this journey together, and so glad that I was athletic, because she had been really trying to become so herself. I was more pleased with me in that moment, in the actualization of my intuition, than I would be for weeks.

But while Erin was cheerful and pleasant, she lacked a certain something that some of her equally affectionate classmates did not. I just couldn't place it, that something. I studied Jane's face, tried to read it. One final embrace from Adam shrouded me briefly in a sweet, sticky smell that I struggled for a moment to identify, but only because of my surroundings. In the embrace's release I caught the scent again. Unmistakable. Marijuana. These homos were high as kites.

Ruth was over with Reverend Rick, who was in his rockstar weekend attire of jeans and a T-shirt, and when we caught glances, he gave me a big smile and a wave. He seemed just the same as he had when he'd visited Gates of Praise. And Ruth wouldn't know this smell if she was handed a joint. If she was handed a bong. Were they all high? Was Pastor Rick high too? I couldn't get a read on Jane. She was talking with the

Cap'n Crunch guy about the group's purchases. A couple of them were already dispersing to their rooms, to the kitchen. *Freedom time*, Jane had said. I would have taken my high outdoors.

Despite how unnatural the movement, I leaned in close to Erin as she listed off various furniture arrangements we might try in our room, *for fun*. I pretended like I was having trouble hearing her. "So you're all about the Vikings, huh?" I asked, inhaling deeply. Nothing except dryer sheet–smelling overalls. "You know it! Don't worry—you'll get decoration privileges soon. Maybe you'll become a Vikings fan in the meantime." Erin started up a lengthy question-and-answer session, and for the second time that day, it was Jane who played my rescuer.

She was just so authentic with that clipboard. "Sorry, you two," she said. "Rick needs to meet with your aunt. He said I should finish showing you around."

I thought that I was done with Jane as semi-disinterested tour guide, but seeing the clipboard, the implied authority of the good preacher, and Erin was off to our room. She couldn't wait, though, she told me, until we could *just gab and gab.*

Jane said something to Reverend Rick. He nodded at me again, everything just so, well, cool, relaxed. Then Jane took me to the hayloft of the main barn. She struggled climbing the ladder, its wood old and gray, but she struggled like it was a common thing. I could tell she came here often. Me a townie kid and always discovering things of such importance in barns.

"So now you've met your fellow sinners," Jane said as she motioned for me to sit at the loft's edge, which I did, while she settled in next to me. She had to put her hand against a post to do it, but she was surprisingly nimble. Everything was surprising: Jane, the place itself. "Any thoughts, observations?"

I just went for it. Why not? "Were they *all* high?" I asked as our legs swung free over the edge, Jane's with that squeak every second and a half or so.

She laughed a small laugh. "Good for you," she said. "It's not everyone—there's actually only a few of us repeat offenders."

"So you too?"

"Yeah. Me included. You didn't think Erin was one, didja?" Jane did this little smile, but not at me. Out at the barn.

"No. I figured that out pretty quick." I flicked pieces of hay over the edge just to watch them flutter and sail. "Doesn't Reverend Rick catch on? A couple of them smelled like they came straight from Woodstock."

"He can't smell. Not at all. He hasn't ever been able to—since birth. You'll hear all about it. He loves to find meaning in his not being able to smell." Jane flashed a quick picture of some falling hay. She used that camera like a whip.

"What about everybody else?"

"You just met them. They don't need to get high. God is the best high, right?" Jane actually hooked my eyes to hers with that line. But she wouldn't let them stay that way.

"Why don't they tell on you?"

She smiled to herself again. "Sometimes they do."

"What does that mean?"

"You'll see. Whatever you think this place is, you'll be in for a surprise. I mean it. You just have to be here for a while and you'll understand."

"It's not like I have a choice," I said. "I'm stuck here. This is where I am."

"Then I'm guessing you'll want in."

"With what?"

"The pot," Jane said, so matter-of-factly.

I hadn't thought it would be this easy. Or maybe it wouldn't be easy at all, but she had offered. "Absolutely," I said.

"Do you have any money?"

"Some," I said. We weren't supposed to bring any money with us; that was in the manual. But I'd rolled about $500 worth of lifeguarding cash and leftover bills from Dad's dresser drawer, twenties and fifties, into tight little bundles barely thicker than chopsticks, and I'd hidden those in various locations throughout my luggage, so that even if some of them were found, others might escape.

Jane was messing with the straps and buckles on her leg, pulling at things. It was grossing me out. The stump was all covered with a brace and padding, but I was afraid that if she didn't stop messing with it soon, it wouldn't be.

She noticed me noticing this. "I keep some of the stash in my leg. I have a little compartment hollowed out. You'll get over it."

"I'm fine with it," I said, throwing lots of hay and not looking.

"No you're not. But you will be after a couple of hits." In her fingers was a baggie with a good amount of pot in it, and also a soapstone pipe.

I was impressed. "I'm impressed," I said.

Jane packed the pipe like someone who had done it plenty of times before, replaced the bag, and pulled forth a red Bic. "I'm resourceful. I'm actually a bit of an off-the-land type, you know? I was born in a barn."

It seemed like the setup for a punch line. "Oh yeah. You and Jesus."

"Exactly," she told me, exhaling, passing the pipe.

It was strong but harsh, potent is maybe the word, though not necessarily enjoyable going in. My eyes watered immediately.

"You'll get used to it," Jane said as I hacked like a sick cat. "I do the best I can for what's essentially ditch weed."

I nodded at her, squinting, and tried again, let the smoke fill me up while closing my eyes, passing her the pipe before letting myself fall back into the hay. "Where do you guys buy from?"

"From me. I grow it a couple of miles from here, just enough to last us the winter. If we're careful," she added before sucking in again.

I propped myself up on my elbow and studied her as she held in the smoke. "No shit? You're the resident weed farmer?"

She passed the bowl again and settled herself down in the hay with me. "I just told you; I'm an off-the-land type."

"So how'd you end up here?"

Jane raised her eyebrows in what I guessed was supposed to be a mysterious way. "The tabloids," she said, offering nothing else.

"Like because of your name?" I asked.

"Sort of. Not exactly."

Jane was relishing this moment, I could tell. She'd been around long enough to see new students come to Promise and leave Promise, and she knew exactly what I was looking for: her story, her past, the sequence of events that had led her to this place to be saved, just like me. Something about being sent to Promise made me desperate to hear her tell it, to hear all the stories of all the students, right up to the part where their parents, their aunts, whoever, drove down that road and into the parking lot to drop them off. I don't know why the desperation, exactly. I still don't know. Maybe it was feeling like we all had shared history, somehow. That understanding somebody else's path to Promise would help me make sense of my own. What I know is that all of us, *all of us*, collected each other's pasts and shared them, like trading Garbage Pail Kids cards—each one wackier and stranger and more unlikely than the next. But I don't think anybody's ever quite trumped Jane's. Her whole story was suspended in the thick fog of strong pot and a hot August afternoon in a hayloft, so the way I remember things, and the way she told them, might not be one and the same. But that doesn't matter so much as the realization I had while she was telling it—namely that my own past maybe wasn't nearly so movie-of-the-week as a lifetime in Miles City had convinced me it was.

• • •

Jane was raised until the age of eleven on a commune just north of Chubbuck, Idaho. The way she told it, it was as if roadies for the Grateful Dead had crossed with some Amish, and this place was the result. It was good land, left to one of the founders by a grandfather. The commune citizens dug crystals of quartz and amethyst out of the ground, polished them up, sold them at touristy gem shops or art fairs. They grew corn and carrots, Idaho potatoes for sure, and hunted deer and elk. Jane's mother was a beauty, a dark-haired woman from New Mexico, and she was the commune's princess, loved by all. And given all that loving, Jane had two dads.

At a place like that, Jane told me, paternity tests meant nothing. Who can truly claim ownership of a soul? Of a life? Shit like that. One possible father was Rishel—the commune mechanic with watery eyes and a slouchy walk and always a roll of all-cherry Life Savers in his back pocket. The other possibility was Gabe. He was some sort of professor. He'd work at a community college for a semester teaching literature and poetry and then spend the next semester on the commune. He rode a Vespa and had a little beard, smoked a Sherlock Holmes pipe mainly as a prop.

Somehow those men, who in high school might have slunk away from one another in an empty hallway, found respect for each other out there on that commune. Or at least something like respect. The naming of the baby was only a minor roadblock.

Rishel wanted Jane, for his mother: a wedding-cake maker from Chubbuck who had put her head in her bakery's oven after finishing a five-tier. Gabe wanted Jane for, you guessed it, his own mother: a breast cancer–surviving meter maid from Saratoga. And there was no question of the last name, Jane would take her mother's, and it was Fonda, and they had all enjoyed

Barbarella (for varying reasons—Gabe: ironically; Rishel: genuinely), so there you go. Jane Fonda it was.

Gabe called the name a triumph of postmodernism.

Rishel called the name simple and straightforward. Plain.

A good choice.

Jane Fonda was born in the commune barn in December, with a retired ER nurse named Pat pulling her free. Pat was apparently the nurse straight outta *Romeo and Juliet*, loud and self-assured, with a mass of gray braids and pink hands like slices of ham. Pat and her lover, Candace, a retired cop, had recently moved to the commune to spend their pensions toward the good of the whole. Before Idaho they'd lived on one of the lesbian separatist Womyn's Lands in Southern California, owned and run by several of Berkeley's Gutter Dykes. Pat and Candace had enjoyed their time in a womyn–only utopia until they'd headed to Canada for a folk festival, stopped to see friends in Chubbuck, and just never quite made it back.

Pat and Jane Fonda were close. Then Pat died in a snowmobile accident, the same accident during which

Jane mangled her leg. So in one afternoon, there went her leg, from the knee down, and there went her nurse and role model. Gabe hadn't been back on the commune for maybe two years before that, and Rishel never knew quite what to say about tragedy without still sounding like *The Farmer's Almanac*.

Not on the night of Jane's birth, not at all, but later, Jane's mother would glean from the evening all kinds of Christian significance. The manger, the month, the bright starry night, even the trio of wise-ass commune musicians plucking out tunes to birth by and passing around a pie for all to share. No one could ever quite get straight why Jane was born in a barn in the first place. They had a couple of cabins, several warm tepees.

"Because it was God's hand," Jane's mom had later decided. Jane's mom was sticking with that.

WORLD
BOOK
DAY

SPONSORED BY
NATIONAL
BOOK
tokens

#ReadingisPower

Whatever the time of day, morning, noon or night, there's always time to discover and share stories. You can . . .

1 PAY A VISIT to your LOCAL BOOKSHOP

A treasure trove of books to browse and choose, you'll also find excellent tips and reading recommendations from helpful booksellers, and lots of book-themed events to enjoy.

 FIND YOUR LOCAL BOOKSHOP: booksellers.org.uk/ bookshopsearch

2 JOIN your LOCAL LIBRARY

So many books to browse and borrow – entirely for free! Get advice on what to read next, and take part in their brilliant free activities.

 FIND YOUR LOCAL LIBRARY: gov.uk/local-library -services/

3 GO TO the **WORLD BOOK DAY** WEBSITE

If you need inspiration, reading and writing tips, ideas or resources, **worldbookday.com** is packed with fun and exciting podcasts, videos, activities, interviews with your favourite authors and illustrators, all the latest book news and much more.

Celebrate stories. Love reading.

World Book Day is a registered charity.

WORLD
**BOOK
DAY**

SPONSORED BY
NATIONAL
**BOOK
tokens**

READING IS POWER

- What's the **GREATEST BOOK** you've ever read, the most **POWERFUL STORY** ever told?

- Which **AUTHOR** speaks to you the loudest, who is the **CHARACTER** that **STUCK IN YOUR HEAD** long after you put the book down?

- Which **ILLUSTRATORS** enchant you and make you want to pick up a pen yourself?

- How do you get your **BOOKISH** fix? Downloaded to your phone or do you prefer the feel of a book in your hands?

How do *you* share stories?

Here at World Book Day, **we celebrate books in all their glory and guises**, we love to **think and talk about books**. Did you know we are a **charity**, here to bring books, your favourite **authors and illustrators** and much more to readers like you?

We believe **BOOKS AND READING ARE A GIFT,** and this book is our gift to **YOU.**

#ShareAStory today, in celebration of all the books you love